Disney's
COUNTDOWN TO
EXTINCTION

A. J. Wood

Illustrated by
Chris Forsey

DISNEP
PRESS

New York

Everyone knows what dinosaurs look like. Or do they?

After all, nobody has ever actually seen a dinosaur. Or they hadn't until the Dinosaur Institute invented the Time Rover. Now, thanks to this transdimensional time-travel machine, we can journey back to the past – the prehistoric past to be precise!

So climb aboard and join us on a ride through time and space, to a time many millions of years ago when giant reptiles ruled the earth.

Our mission?

To check up on seven prehistoric creatures and update the Institute's computer records.

Our problem?

To avoid the pitfalls of prehistoric life: erupting volcanoes, exploding meteors, and most of all, hungry dinosaurs!

So grab your notebook, climb aboard, and start the countdown – **your journey back in time is about to begin...**

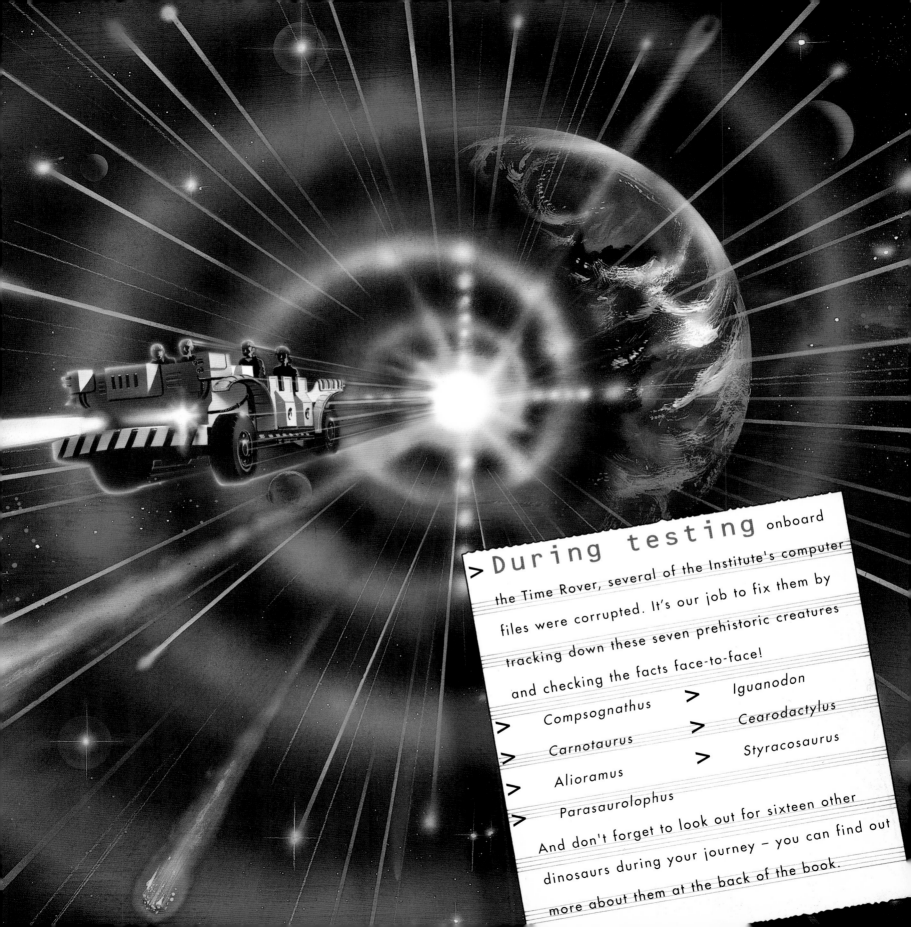

> **During testing** onboard the Time Rover, several of the Institute's computer files were corrupted. It's our job to fix them by tracking down these seven prehistoric creatures and checking the facts face-to-face!

> Compsognathus   > Iguanodon

> Carnotaurus   > Cearodactylus

> Alioramus   > Styracosaurus

> Parasaurolophus

And don't forget to look out for sixteen other dinosaurs during your journey – you can find out more about them at the back of the book.

> Name: *Compsognathus*

> Time: Late Jurassic Period

> Place: Western Europe

The Time Rover has safely transported us on the first leg of our journey, back 150 million years or so to a rocky ravine in what is now France. We know from fossil records that the dinosaurs ruled the planet for 130 million years. By around 150 million years ago, during a time known as the Jurassic Period, species of all shapes and sizes dominated the earth. Many had developed elaborate spines or crests like the *Dacentrurus* shown here; others grew to giant proportions. One of the biggest dinosaurs of all time, *Brachiosaurus*, lived during this period and grew to a towering 52 feet (16 meters) in height. But if you thought that all dinosaurs were huge, here's a flock of chicken-sized ones to prove you wrong.

The first dinosaur that we need to check on, *Compsognathus,* was a tiny, fast-footed hunter that lived on lizards and insects. And it looks like this flock needs to be fast if it's going to escape from being squashed in this meteor shower! Looking closely at this scene should help you identify two mistakes in the Institute's Dinofile.

D I N O F I L E

> Name: *Compsognathus* (KOMP-sog-NAY-thus)

> Size: 98 feet (30 meters)

> Diet: Insects and small vertebrates

> Description: *Compsognathus* was a fast-running predator, agile and speedy enough to catch prey such as lizards.
One of the smallest known dinosaurs, its long tail would have helped to balance its body when running and its five-fingered hands and sharp teeth were useful for grasping prey.

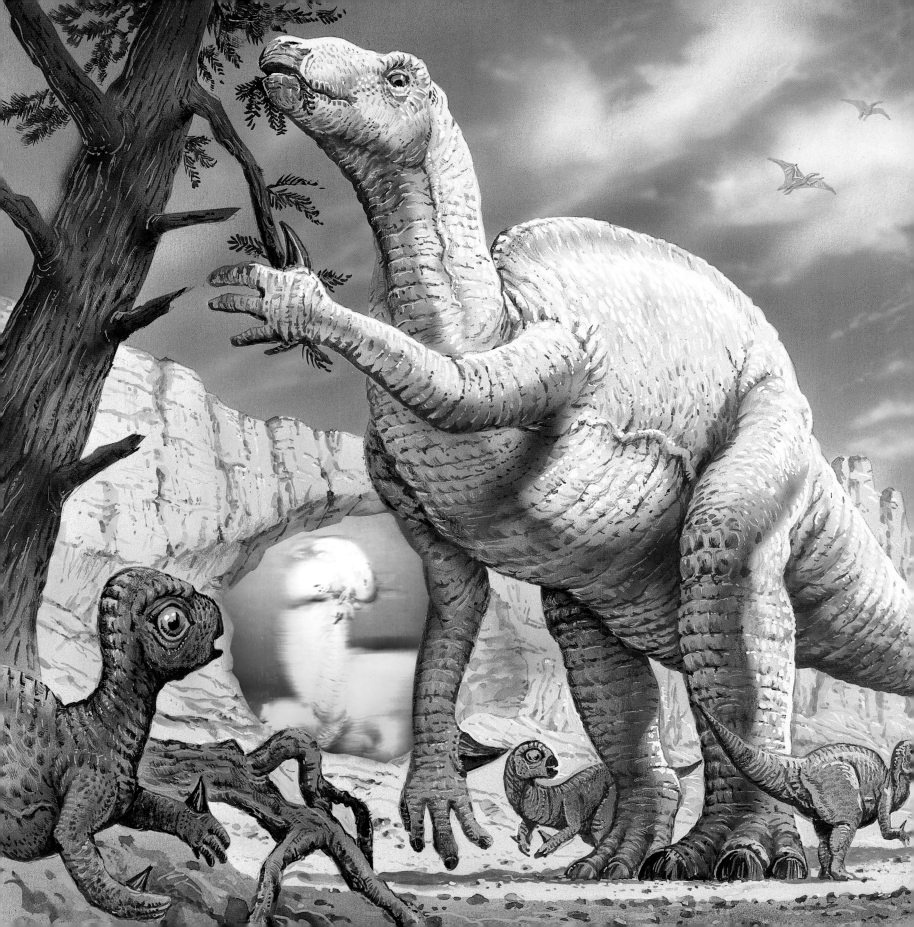

> Name: Iguanodon (I-gwan-uh-don)

> Size: 33 feet (10 meters)

> Diet: Plants

> Description: Well adapted to its carnivorous diet, the Iguanodon had a beaklike mouth, with strong jaws and a powerful tongue, ideal for biting off and swallowing plant matter. Its hands and feet featured a large spike that may have been useful in defense but was more likely used to rake tree branches down to its mouth.

120 million
years ago

> Name: *Iguanodon*

> Time: Early Cretaceous Period

> Place: Western Europe

A leap forward in time by a mere 30 million years brings us to the Cretaceous Period, when the dinosaurs really came into their own. They covered the land in an even greater variety and with more advanced designs than ever before. New types of plants were beginning to evolve and, alongside them, new types of plant-eating dinosaurs. Our second dinosaur – *Iguanodon* – was one of these.

We know from fossil remains that this creature was very common in many parts of the prehistoric world, and the large collections of skeletons that have been unearthed have led scientists to think that *Iguanodon* may have lived in herds. Its young would have hatched from a clutch of eggs, probably laid in a dirt nest made by scraping earth into a mound. They may well have been cared for by their parents for some time after hatching.

Iguanodon was one of the first dinosaurs ever to be discovered, when its fossilized teeth were found in a pile of roadside gravel way back in 1822. Before you move on to discover your next dinosaur, don't forget to check the facts in the Dinofile and look for two other dinosaur species that lived alongside the interesting *Iguanodon* – *Ornithopsis* and *Polacanthus*.

> Name: *Carnotaurus*

> Time: Middle Cretaceous Period

> Place: South America

At 25 feet (7.5 meters) long, and with a head full of saw-edged teeth, our third dinosaur, the mean meat-eating *Carnotaurus,* is one creature you wouldn't want to mess with. Its name means "meat-eating bull." Given its fearsome nature, *Carnotaurus* probably did not need to use the horns above its eyes as weapons; instead they were most likely used to attract a mate or to intimidate a rival of its own kind.

This prehistoric predator was armed with a mouthful of strong teeth and, judging by the way that this *Carnotaurus* is gnashing his, it might be a good time to move on in search of more dinosaurs. But before we return to the Rover in search of the next species on our list, can you spot another dinosaur sharing its home with the carnivorous *Carnotaurus?*

DINOFILE

> Name: Carnotaurus (KAHR-nuh-TOR-us)

> Size: 2.5 feet (1 meter)

> Diet: Meat; capable of catching and swallowing other animals as big as humans

> Description: Slim, scaly body with small, short arms and long legs; bull-like head with flat horns sticking out from side used to catch and kill prey; rough skin covered in bony bumps. Fossil remains also tell us that this dinosaur most likely had exceptional eyesight, useful in hunting for food.

> Name: *Cearadactylus*

> Time: Late Cretaceous Period

> Place: Coastal North America

Now for something completely different – the Rover has tracked down a mother *Cearadactylus* and her nest of young. These creatures weren't actually dinosaurs at all, but flying reptiles known as pterosaurs. Like the dinosaurs and the giant sea-dwelling reptiles, pterosaurs mysteriously died out around 65 million years ago. At least we've made it back in time to check out what a live *Cearadactylus* looks like, even if this one's a bit close for comfort...

Pterosaurs ranged in size from tiny, sparrowlike creatures to aerial giants with a wing span of up to 50 feet (15 meters). Many had beaks edged with small, spiky teeth and huge claws at the ends of their fingers and toes. Can you spot the largest flying reptile of all, *Quetzalcoatlus,* and some *Pteranodons* sharing the prehistoric skies with *Cearadactylus?* They'd better all watch out – there's an egg-eating *Ornithomimus* lurking nearby as well.

DINOFILE

> Name: *Cearadactylus* (SEE-ra-DACK-til-US)

> Size: 18 feet (5.5 meters)

> Diet: Fish

> Description: An albatross of the prehistoric world, this pterosaur would have soared over oceans and lakes in its search for food. Its pointed beak, armed with powerful dentition, could catch the most slippery fish; the front teeth were particularly long. The wing claws were also long to assist in holding prey.

> Name: *Alioramus*

> Time: Late Cretaceous Period

> Place: Asia

Thanks to the Time Rover, we've now zoomed even further forward in time to see what planet Earth looked like a mere 70 million years ago, and our search has led us into the heart of a primeval forest in what is now Mongolia. Our fifth prehistoric creature, the ever-hungry *Alioramus*, evolved toward the end of the Cretaceous Period and was a member of one of the last and most advanced group of meat-eating dinosaurs – the tyrannosaurids. Like its relatives, *Alioramus* was perfectly designed for hunting, with its strong, muscular legs and heavy head.

Looking closely at this *Alioramus* should help you identify two mistakes in the Institute's Dinofile. And don't forget to look for three other dinosaurs lurking elsewhere in the jungle – *Velociraptor*, *Protoceratops,* and *Oviraptor.*

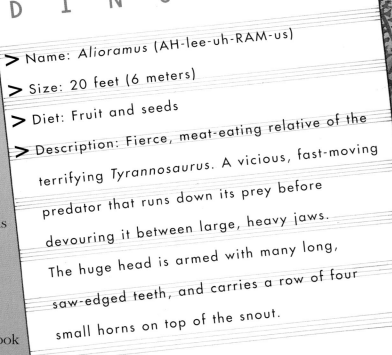

D I N O F I L E

> Name: *Alioramus* (AH-lee-uh-RAM-us)

> Size: 20 feet (6 meters)

> Diet: Fruit and seeds

> Description: Fierce, meat-eating relative of the terrifying *Tyrannosaurus*. A vicious, fast-moving predator that runs down its prey before devouring it between large, heavy jaws. The huge head is armed with many long, saw-edged teeth, and carries a row of four small horns on top of the snout.

> Name: *Styracosaurus*

> Time: Late Cretaceous Period

> Place: North America

By the end of the Age of Dinosaurs many of the plants that we know today were growing on the earth. Forests of trees and many types of flowering plants covered the land. Plants provided food for a whole host of prehistoric herbivores. Our third dinosaur, *Styracosaurus,* was one of these. The long spikes protruding from its bony neck frill might make *Styracosaurus* look fierce, but they were most likely used to prevent this dinosaur from becoming someone else's lunch! *Styracosaurus,* like its bigger relative *Triceratops,* may also have used its remarkable headgear to threaten rivals and attract mates.

It would be hard to miss the two other dinosaurs sharing their home with *Styracosaurus* – the terrible *Tyrannosaurus* and the towering *Triceratops.* Do you know which is which?

DINOFILE

> Name: *Styracosaurus* (stye-RACK-uh-SAW-rus)

> Period: Late Cretaceous

> Size: 18 feet (5.25 meters)

> Diet: Insects

> Description: A relative of *Tyrannosaurus,* *Styracosaurus* probably roamed in herds, browsing on low-growing plants. This well-armored dinosaur had a bony neck frill supporting four long spikes. These, together with its nasal horn, may have been used to frighten predators or in fighting for territory or mates.

> Name: *Parasaurolophus*

> Time: Late Cretaceous Period

> Place: North America

By the Late Cretaceous Period there were a huge number of dinosaur species roaming the earth. Think of the variety of animals alive today and you can be pretty sure that there was a dinosaur equivalent – rhinoceroslike plant-eaters such as *Triceratops*, meat-eating "lions" like *Tyrannosaurus*, herds of hadrosaurs wandering across the prehistoric plains like modern-day deer, even tiny lizardlike dinosaurs. Dinosaurs came in all shapes and sizes and many had elaborate horns, spikes, or other unusual features such as the curious nasal crest belonging to our final dinosaur – the hadrosaur *Parasaurolophus.*

This bony tube protruded up to 3.5 feet (1 meter) from the back of its head and may have been used to help amplify its voice – when it was calling out to other dinosaurs, either as a warning of danger or when trying to attract a mate. Its crest would not have been much use as a weapon and, despite its huge size – 30 feet (9 meters) from head to tail, this gentle plant-eater could have been prey for fierce meat-eating dinosaurs, such as this pack of *Dromaeosauruses.*

Before we return to the Rover, can you identify three other dinosaurs visiting this prehistoric water hole – *Edmontosaurus, Albertosaurus,* and *Pachycephalosaurus?*

D I N O F I L E

> Name: *Parasaurolophus*
(PAR-uh-SAW-ruh-LOH-fus)

> Period: Late Cretaceous

> Size: 2.5 feet (1 meter)

> Diet: Plants

> Description: Would have walked on all fours when browsing on low-growing plants, but ran on its two hind legs. The most prominent feature of this hadrosaur was its bony head crest, which was probably used to help it breathe underwater.

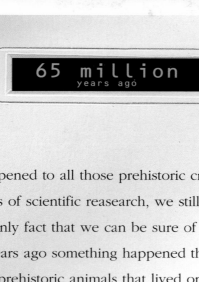

So what happened to all those prehistoric creatures? Despite years of scientific reasearch, we still don't really know. The only fact that we can be sure of is that around 65 million years ago something happened that wiped out all the large prehistoric animals that lived on Earth.

Scientists have guessed that the dinosaurs were killed off by the effects of an asteroid collision, the spread of some powerful disease, or some other great catastrophe. We do know that after the dinosaurs had ruled the planet for over 140 million years, their disappearance left the stage clear for smaller creatures – such as mammals – to step into the limelight. And so they did. In a matter of just a few million years the mammals evolved into a huge array of species, from large land-living animals such as rhinos and mammoths to sea creatures such as whales and dolphins, and high fliers such as bats. It took another 60 or so million years for the first humans to appear, yet in the short time we've been around we've changed the face of planet Earth more than any other species.

Our mission is complete. We've checked our files and it's time to **set the controls for the twentieth century – we're ready to go home!**

What we know now:

Now it's time to update the Dinosaur Institute's information files with the facts on our seven prehistoric creatures. That's providing you remembered to make notes. You didn't? Well, lucky for you, we did – and you can read them below. The earliest dinosaurs first appeared in the Triassic Period, nearly 200 million years ago. Over the 130 million years that followed they developed into many different types. You can see some of them, and their airborne relatives, here.

UPDATES

> *Compsognathus:* This dinosaur was only as big as a chicken, measuring approximately 40 inches (1 meter) in length; it only had three fingers on its hands, not five.

> *Iguanodon:* This dinosaur was a herbivore, not a carnivore. One of the ways we can tell this is by looking at fossilized remains of its teeth. Several of these were found by Mary Mantell in England, in 1922. Her husband, Gideon, an amateur geologist, incorrectly deduced that they were the remains of a giant prehistoric lizard, an extinct relative of the modern-day iguana. He named the creature *Iguanodon,* meaning "iguana-tooth." *Iguanodon* had a large thumb spike on its hands but not on its feet.

> *Carnotaurus:* Measured 25 feet (7.5 meters); its horns were probably used in display rather than to catch prey.

> *Cearadactylus:* Its beak was rounded at the tip rather than pointed.

> *Alioramus:* Ate meat, not fruits and seeds; had six horns on its snout, not four.

> *Styracosaurus:* Ate plants rather than insects; was a relative of *Triceratops,* not *Tyrannosaurus;* had six spikes protruding from its neck frill, not four.

> *Parasaurolophus:* Measured 30 feet (9 meters); although scientists once believed that its crest enabled this dinosaur to breathe underwater, we now know that this is untrue.

> **1** *Dacentrurus*
A relative of *Stegosaurus* and the first stegosaur fossil ever discovered.

> **2** *Ornithopsis*
This giant of the prehistoric world lived only on plants.

> **3** *Polacanthus*
This armored plant-eater had protective spines along its sides.

> **4** *Saltasaurus*
Like *Ornithopsis,* this dinosaur would have grazed on plant matter from the tops of trees. It lived alongside *Carnotaurus.*

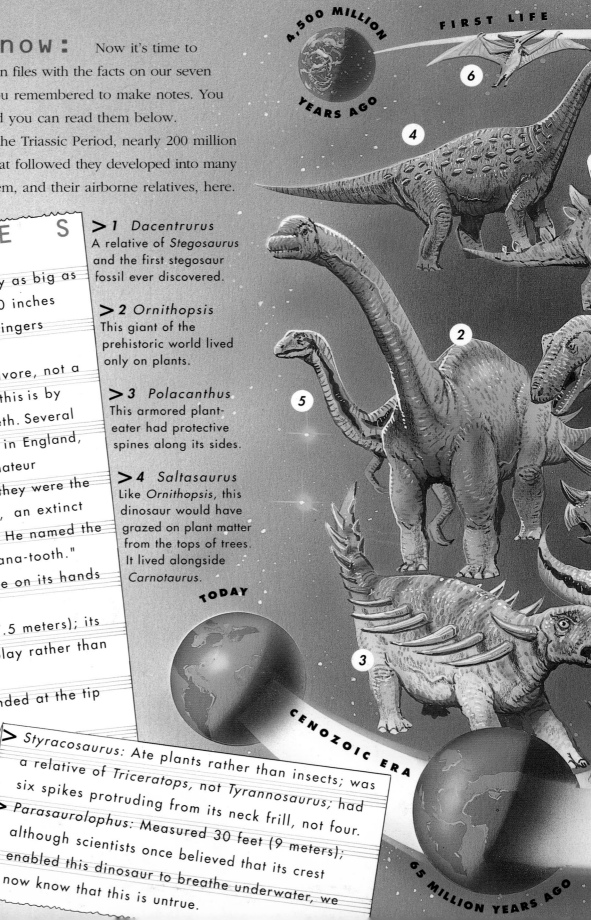

4,500 MILLION YEARS AGO

FIRST LIFE

TODAY

CENOZOIC ERA

65 MILLION YEARS AGO